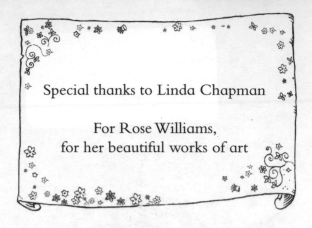

Special thanks to Linda Chapman

For Rose Williams,
for her beautiful works of art

ORCHARD BOOKS
338 Euston Road, London NW1 3BH
Orchard Books Australia
Level 17/207 Kent Street, Sydney, NSW 2000
A Paperback Original

First published in 2015 by Orchard Books

Text © Hothouse Fiction Limited 2015

Illustrations © Orchard Books 2015

A CIP catalogue record for this book is available
from the British Library.

ISBN 978 1 40833 285 6

1 3 5 7 9 10 8 6 4 2

Printed in Great Britain

The paper and board used in this book are made from wood from responsible sources.

Orchard Books is a division of Hachette Children's Books,
an Hachette UK company

www.hachette.co.uk

Series created by Hothouse Fiction
www.hothousefiction.com

Sparkle Statue

ROSIE BANKS

ORCHARD

This is the Secret Kingdom

Magnificent Museum

Contents

A Magic Message

Ellie Macdonald concentrated hard as she made the final touches to the pixie she was painting. She added a shimmer of glitter paint to the green ring on the pixie's finger and sat back. "Finished!" she said happily.

Summer Hammond and Jasmine Smith, her two best friends, looked up.

They were all painting pictures for a
display at Honeyvale Library. Summer
was drawing a unicorn and Jasmine had
almost finished a mermaid.

"Oh, wow, Ellie! That's brilliant," said
Summer. "It looks just like Trixi."

Ellie grinned. "It's much easier to paint
a pixie when you're friends with one!"

The three girls giggled. They shared
an amazing secret – they actually knew
real pixies, unicorns and mermaids! They
looked after the Magic Box, which could
take them to an amazing place called
the Secret Kingdom, where all kinds of
magical creatures lived! Their best friends
there were King Merry, the land's kind
ruler, and Trixibelle, his royal pixie.

Summer sighed. "I may have seen lots
of unicorns, but my picture still looks

more like a camel!"

"And my mermaid is nowhere near as beautiful as a real mermaid," Jasmine said, showing her picture to Ellie. "What should I do?"

"Her face is really pretty," Ellie said. "But her purple tail doesn't look quite right…" She studied the painting. "I know! Why don't you add some different colours to the scales on her tail to make them shimmer?"

"Good idea," said Jasmine. "I'll try that."

"What about my unicorn, Ellie?" Summer asked eagerly.

Ellie pointed at the unicorn's back with her paintbrush. "Try picturing a unicorn in your head. Their backs curve down, not up." As she traced a curve in the air

above Summer's
picture, a blob
of glitter
paint fell off
her brush
and landed
on the
unicorn's
tummy.

"I'm so
sorry!" she
gasped.

"Don't worry," said Summer. "I can
start again."

"No, don't do that," Ellie said quickly.
"You can use the glitter to make your
unicorn glow. Like this—" She blended
the glitter into the unicorn's pale pink
tummy then added some to the unicorn's

mane and legs. Then she handed the
brush to Summer. "Here, you try."

"My mermaid looks better already,"
said Jasmine, smiling at her picture.
"You're so good at art, Ellie."

"We're all good at different things.
You're amazing at singing and dancing,"
said Ellie.

Jasmine grinned. "And Summer's
brilliant with animals – even magical
ones!"

"Oh, I miss the Secret Kingdom," Ellie
said longingly. "It's been ages since we
had a new adventure there. Should we
check the Magic Box? There might be a
message from Trixi and King Merry. Did
you bring it, Summer?"

"Of course!" Summer picked up her
bag and handed it to Ellie.

Ellie was just about to open the drawstring top when her little sister, Molly, came running into the kitchen. Ellie hastily covered the bag with her arms so Molly couldn't see it.

"Look at my painting!" Molly cried. She held up a drawing of a lopsided stick figure, covered in glitter.

"It's really good, Molly," Summer said encouragingly. "What is it?"

"It's a fairy, silly!" said Molly, as if Summer should have known. She waved it around so that the glitter caught the rays of sun streaming in through the kitchen window. "Look at it sparkle!"

As Ellie leaned down over the backpack, her eyes were caught by another sparkle – coming from inside the bag! She caught her breath and opened the drawstring top just a little way. The wooden box inside was glowing – there must be a message for them! She hastily shut the bag. The Secret Kingdom had to be kept a secret, so they couldn't look in front of Molly.

"You know what, Mol?" she said. "I think you should paint a big, glittery yellow sun on your picture and maybe add some really sparkly birds in the sky."

"More glitter?" Molly asked eagerly.

"Yes, lots more," said Ellie, nodding hard. "I have some special *glitter* gel pens in my bedroom you can borrow." She saw Summer and Jasmine looking at her as if she'd gone mad. Ellie knew her little sister would make a mess, but it was worth it if it meant she and her friends could go on an adventure in the

Secret Kingdom! "Make your picture really *glow*," she said, winking at the others and nodding her head towards her backpack.

Instantly their faces lit up and she knew they'd understood.

"Yes, you should add *loads* more glitter," Jasmine said.

Molly skipped off happily.

As soon as the kitchen door shut behind her, Summer and Jasmine jumped to their feet. "Is there a message for us?" Jasmine asked breathlessly.

"Yes!" Ellie pulled open the bag, revealing the box glowing inside. Golden light shone out into the kitchen as words swirled across the mirrored lid.

They knelt down on the floor and Summer took out the Magic Box.

Jasmine read out the message:

"To my friends, I send a magic invite
To celebrate art that sparkles so bright.
Find statues and paintings and all
kinds of fun,
In a place full of beauty for everyone!"

As Jasmine finished speaking, the box opened and a map floated out.

But Ellie wasn't looking at the map. Something else had caught her eye. "Wow! Look at these!" she exclaimed in delight, peering into the Magic Box.

Summer and Jasmine looked over her shoulder. Inside the Magic Box there were four friendship bracelets. One was purple, one was hot pink, one was yellow and one – a very tiny one – was green. They each had a pretty silver charm attached.

"They're friendship bracelets!" said Jasmine in surprise.

Summer carefully lifted the friendship bracelets out of the Magic Box. "Do you think they're for us?"

"Well, they *are* in all our favourite

colours," Ellie said thoughtfully.

"Oh and look!" Jasmine held up a tiny
bracelet in leaf green. "This little one
would be just right for Trixi."

Summer examined the silver charms.
The charm on the pink bracelet was a
musical note, the charm on the purple

bracelet was a paintbrush, the yellow bracelet had a paw print charm and the tiny green one had a leaf charm. "They *must* be for us!" she said.

"Maybe King Merry put them in there to replace all the things we lost," said Jasmine. Until recently, all the box's compartments had contained different magical items, but most of them had been broken the last time the girls had defeated Queen Malice – the king's horrid sister – when she had tried to take over the Secret Kingdom.

They each took their friendship bracelet and slipped it on.

"It was so lovely of King Merry to give us these," said Summer, admiring their bracelets.

"Well, what are we waiting for?"

said Jasmine with a grin. "Let's solve the riddle so we can go to the Secret Kingdom and thank him!"

A Royal Portrait

Ellie felt a thrill of excitement as she looked at the magical map of the crescent-shaped Secret Kingdom. Unicorns cantered through a lush, green valley, fluffy snow bears rolled down the frosty slopes of Magic Mountain, and giant water snails swam through the sparkling waters of Lily Pad Lake.

"The riddle says we need to go to a place where you'd find a painting or a statue," Jasmine said, gazing down at the map.

"That's easy," Ellie said. "You find paintings and statues in a museum."

Jasmine nodded. "That makes sense. But does the Secret Kingdom have a museum?"

Summer studied the map carefully. "There!" she cried, pointing to a pink building with lots of pillars. "That's where we need to go." A sign outside the building read "King Merry's Magnificent Museum".

Placing their hands on the jewels on top of the Magic Box, Jasmine, Ellie and Summer called out together, "King Merry's Magnificent Museum!"

There was a bright flash of light and then a small green blur whizzed past the girls' noses. It whooshed to a stop and turned into Trixi, a tiny royal pixie standing on a green leaf. She was wearing a short silver dress with matching boots and had a little hat that looked like a daisy on her short blonde hair. "Hello, girls!" she said, kissing each of them on the nose. "I'm glad you got my message so quickly."

"We got the friendship bracelets too," said Summer.

Trixi looked confused. "What friendship bracelets?"

"These ones," said Ellie, showing Trixi her bracelet. "They were in the Magic Box. Look – there's even one for you." She handed Trixi the tiny green bracelet.

Trixi eagerly put it on and held out her arm to admire it. "Oh! King Merry must have forgotten to tell me about them. He's so forgetful! But isn't it lovely of him to get us all presents?"

"I really like mine," said Jasmine, admiring the hot-pink bracelet with the musical note.

"Is Queen Malice causing trouble again?" Summer asked the little pixie anxiously.

"Oh no," said Trixi. "This time King Merry wants you to visit for fun! It's Talent Week in the Secret Kingdom! It's an ancient and important Secret Kingdom tradition. Every year King Merry presents four magical awards to people whose special talents make the kingdom a particularly lovely place to live. As you are all so talented, the king has invited you to attend the ceremonies and meet the award winners. The first ceremony will be at King Merry's Magnificent Museum. Would you girls like to come?"

Summer and Ellie nodded eagerly, but Jasmine was less keen.

"But museums are usually boring," she said with a sigh.

Trixi giggled. "Museums must be very

different in your world. King Merry's Magnificent Museum is *never* boring!"

Jasmine grinned. "That's true – nothing in the Secret Kingdom is ever dull!"

"Yippee! Then off we go!" Trixi said. She tapped her green ring and chanted:

*"Magic pixie ring, please whisk us away
To the museum for a wonderful day!"*

A burst of golden light shot out of the ring and surrounded the girls. They felt themselves being slowly lifted off the ground and then they spun away.

They landed outside a huge building with pink walls and tall pillars carved with pictures of unicorns, mermaids, elves and pixies.

As the cloud of magic sparkles slowly

cleared, Summer put her hand up and smiled as she felt her tiara nestled on her head. She and her friends had special tiaras that appeared when they arrived in the Secret Kingdom. They showed everyone in the realm that they were King Merry's Very Important Friends.

"King Merry's having his portrait painted by the famous painter, Jasper Rococo," Trixi told them. "We can go into the museum but we'd better be quiet – Jasper hates being disturbed when he's painting." Trixi put her finger to her lips.

Pulling open the heavy, carved doors, the girls entered an enormous gallery. The ceiling was made of glass, and sunlight streamed down onto the paintings and statues dotted all around.

At one end of the gallery, King Merry was perched on a throne, his little legs dangling down. An artist wearing a smock and a feathered beret was standing in front of an easel, adding brush strokes to the portrait he was painting. There was a table next to him covered in brushes and paints in all the colours of the rainbow.

King Merry was holding the Secret
Spellbook, the ancient magic book that
belonged to the ruler of the kingdom. His
crown was perched on his curly white
hair and his half-moon spectacles were
slipping down his nose. He started to turn
the book's pages absent-mindedly.

"No, no, no!" the artist exclaimed,

throwing his arms up dramatically. He
had purple hair and a
matching moustache
that turned up
at the ends. "I
have told you
before, you
must not move,
Your Majesty!"
He stabbed the
paintbrush at King
Merry, dripping purple
paint on the floor. "I cannot possibly
paint you if you are going to fidget like
a flea!"

The king sighed. "Crowns and
coronations, Jasper, I'm getting very tired
of sitting still."

The artist set to work again, his

paintbrush moving in a blur. He clicked his fingers and three little creatures with rosy cheeks and pointy ears started racing around the table beside the easel, mixing paints and cleaning brushes. One wore a red smock and had a shock of red hair, another wore all yellow and had hair the colour of lemons, and the third one wore a bright blue smock and had hair the same colour. They reminded Jasmine of a box of crayons!

"What are those?" whispered Jasmine.

"Art imps," said Trixi. "They help Jasper with his painting."

"Ta-da!" Jasper declared, spinning round on the spot. "The painting is finished!"

"Oh, thank goodness for that," said King Merry, wriggling off the throne.

"King Merry!" called Trixi. "Over here!"

"My dears!" King Merry exclaimed. Forgetting all about the painting, he came rushing over to greet them. "Oh, how lovely it is to see you all again!" The girls hugged him but his tummy was so plump that their arms wouldn't fit around him properly.

King Merry chuckled in delight. "Goodness gracious, it's so wonderful that you were able to come."

"Thank you so much for inviting us," said Summer.

"And thank you for our friendship

bracelets," said Ellie, holding hers up.

King Merry frowned. "Friendship bracelets? I didn't give you friendship bracelets."

"But they were in the Magic Box," exclaimed Jasmine.

"How strange," said King Merry,

inspecting Ellie's bracelet. "They are very pretty."

Jasper Rococo cleared his throat noisily. "A-hum! Your Majesty, my painting!" He was looking rather cross and Ellie noticed his moustache had turned red at the ends.

"Oh yes, of course, Jasper," said King Merry. "Do come and see my portrait, girls, and tell me what you think. We can deal with the mystery of these bracelets later."

They all gathered round the easel, where Jasper was proudly displaying the painting. The art imps were rushing around, tidying up Jasper's brushes and cleaning up drips of paint from the floor. They grinned and waved at the girls.

Ellie examined the portrait. It was so

realistic that it was almost like looking at a photograph. "It's amazing," she said.

"Jasper's the best illusionist painter in the entire kingdom," Trixi said.

Jasper's moustache turned a happy shade of pink. "I couldn't do it without my imps' help of course." He bowed in the direction of the tiny art imps, who giggled and bowed back to him.

"What's an *illusionist* painter?" asked Ellie. She knew a lot about art but she'd never heard of one of those before.

"I don't believe they have illusionist painters in the Other Realm." King Merry said.

Jasper chuckled. "Aha, my child, then watch this!" He clicked his fingers and a paintbrush magically appeared in his hand. The pearly white bristles looked

silky soft and glowed with every colour
of the rainbow. With a flourish, Jasper
started waving the brush merrily all over
the portrait. Ellie gasped, wondering if it
would smudge the painting, but it didn't.
The brush just left a fine coating of
sparkles over the whole portrait.

Jasper twirled his moustache. "Let the
illusion begin!"

"Oh, spells and sceptres, this is my
favourite bit," said King Merry in
excitement. "Watch, girls!"

The portrait of King Merry started
to move. The little king in the picture
jumped off his throne and waved at
them.

Ellie, Jasmine and Summer gasped.

"Isn't that incredible?" said Trixi.

"Oh yes," breathed Ellie. She wished

she could make her own pictures do that!

The little king in the painting started to dance a jig. As he spun round he knocked his spellbook out of the picture.

"Whoops-a-daisy!" chuckled King

Merry, picking the book up and handing it back to the little king in the picture. "He's a bit clumsy, Jasper!"

The girls and Trixi bit their lips and

tried not to giggle. The real King Merry was often a bit clumsy, too!

The spellbook disappeared back into the painting. The little king waved and jumped back on to his throne.

"Are you pleased, Your Majesty?" Jasper asked, twirling the ends of his purple moustache.

"I am utterly delighted!" declared King Merry, hanging the painting on the wall. "This portrait shall have pride of place in my museum. Your magical paintings make the Secret Kingdom an even more beautiful place, which is why you have been chosen to receive the first Talent Week award: the Sparkle Statue. The ceremony will be later today."

Jasper's moustache turned a proud, peacock blue. "Thank you!" he said, bowing once more.

"Come and see some of Jasper's other pictures," Trixi said to the girls.

"I'd love to!" Ellie quickly replied.

Jasper beamed at her.

A nearby painting of two snow bear cubs caught Ellie's eye. The cubs waved their paws at her and then started tumbling and play fighting in the snow. Ellie giggled and waved back at them.

Next to it was a picture of a beautiful mermaid sitting on a rock in the middle of a sparkling sea. Jasmine's eyes widened in surprise as the mermaid started brushing her long hair.

"Hello!" the mermaid called to her. "It's a lovely day for a swim!" She dived from the rock and splashed around in the water. Jasmine giggled, wishing that she could join her.

Summer went over to a statue of a baby griffin, made out of pale gold stone. He had the head and wings of an eagle but the body and tail of a lion. To her delight, the little griffin moved too! He yawned, opened his wings wide and gave his golden feathers a shake.

Summer bent down and stroked the griffin's downy head. "You're so cute."

The griffin swished his tail happily and nuzzled his head against Summer.

Trixi landed her leaf on Jasmine's shoulder. "Do you

still think museums are boring?" she asked teasingly.

Jasmine grinned. "Definitely not!"

CRASH!

They all jumped at the sound of a loud thunderclap. The sky above the glass ceiling suddenly darkened and the air turned freezing cold. A familiar cackle rang out.

"Oh no," Ellie breathed. "It's Queen Malice!"

Malice in the Museum

King Merry spun round. "Sister? Where are you?" he demanded angrily.

The cackle rose to a screeching laugh and the bony figure of Queen Malice climbed out of a painting of a tall, snowy mountain. She had snow on the hem of her black dress and icicles hanging from her long thunder staff. Her wild hair frizzed out around her face and her midnight-black eyes glittered coldly.

"Surprised to see me here, brother?" she sneered.

"What do you want?" King Merry said. "Go away! You're not welcome in my Magical Museum!"

"That's not very friendly." The queen turned to the girls and Trixi, putting on a sickly sweet voice. "Ah, look, if it isn't my three favourite humans and their little pixie friend. Do you like your new friendship bracelets?"

"Y…yes," stammered Ellie uneasily.

Queen Malice chortled. "I knew you would. But did *you* know that they came from me?"

"From you?" Jasmine echoed.

"Yes!" the queen cried triumphantly. She held up her staff. Dark sparks shot from the thunderbolt as she hissed a spell:

*"Bracelets now, your curse reveal
Lock on tight, and talents steal!"*

Jasmine gasped as she looked down
at her wrist in horror. Her pretty pink
bracelet had turned to horrid black
metal! Summer, Ellie and Trixi's bracelets

had all changed, too.

Jasmine tried to
pull the bracelet
off, but it was
stuck fast.
"I can't get
it off!" she
wailed.

"I can't
either!" Summer
cried as she
struggled to get her
bracelet off.

"Oh dear," said the queen smugly.
"Don't you like them now? Well, too
bad!"

"What have you done?" demanded
Trixi, tugging at her bracelet frantically.

The queen's eyes glittered nastily. "My

beautiful bracelets will take away your special talents. It was that silly Talent Week that gave me the idea. Those prizes reward talent, but I decided it would be much more fun to take it away. You four have interfered with my plans to take over the kingdom too many times – let's see if you can stop me without your special talents!"

"Whatever you're planning to do, we'll still stop you!" Jasmine said angrily.

"This is ridiculous, sister!" exclaimed King Merry. "Take the bracelets off my friends at once."

"No!" cackled the queen. "I won't!" She swept her staff through the air and black sparks shot out, showering the whole museum. In a flash, all the beautiful colours in the pictures faded to dull shades of boring grey.

Horrified, Ellie looked at the paintings they'd admired just moments before. Now the snow bear cubs were growling and snarling at each other, baring their sharp teeth.

SQUIRT!

Water sprayed out of the mermaid painting and soaked the three girls. "Hey!" cried Jasmine, brushing drops of water off her face. "She just spat water on us!"

Sticking out her tongue, the mermaid dived into the water.

But worst of all, a picture of Queen Malice had replaced Jasper's portrait of King Merry!

"I declare that this museum is no longer King Merry's Magnificent Museum. It is Queen Malice's Museum of Misery now!" Queen Malice announced triumphantly. "As long as my picture hangs in this gallery, this museum will be under my spell!"

"No!" Jasper cried. His moustache was bright red with anger. "You shall not ruin my art!" He strode over to the picture of Queen Malice. "I will repaint the picture of King Merry and break your curse."

"We'll see about that!" snarled Queen

Malice, pointing her thunderstaff. There was a loud crack and Jasper turned to golden stone!

Trixi screamed and the girls all gasped.

"Sister!" cried King Merry, wringing his hands in horror. "What have you done?"

The queen sneered. "Ha! See if you can award him the talent prize now!"

She banged her staff on the floor. There was a clap of thunder that shook the museum and then the wicked queen vanished.

Lost Talents

"What are we going to do?" said Summer, looking around the museum in dismay. The art imps were crying as they huddled by the statue of Jasper. The statue moved sadly, shaking his head from side to side as he tried to comfort the little imps.

"Oh, this is quite dreadful," said King Merry wringing his hands. "Why does my horrible sister always have to try and ruin things? Soon everyone will be arriving for the award ceremony. Only, instead of getting a statue, Jasper's been turned into one!"

Jasmine went over to Jasper and touched his marble arm. It felt cold and hard. "Poor Jasper," she said sadly. "Don't worry, we'll fix this."

The statue nodded sadly.

"Queen Malice said the museum will be cursed as long as her picture is hanging here," said Ellie thoughtfully. "So let's just take it down."

The three girls ran over to the picture of Queen Malice and tried to lift it off the wall. But it didn't budge.

"Oh no!" Summer cried in frustration. "It's stuck fast to the wall."

"We need to try something else," said Jasmine. She spotted Jasper's paints and brushes by the wailing art imps. It gave her an idea. "Jasper said he would repaint the picture – Ellie, do you think you could do it?"

"I'll try," said Ellie, nodding. "Please may I use these paints?" she asked the art imps.

The art imps agreed. The one with the bright yellow hair squirted paint from tubes onto Jasper's palette, while the art imp with red hair tied a smock around Ellie. A blue-haired imp handed her a paintbrush and stood on tiptoe to talk to her. "Please help Jasper," he whispered.

"I'll do my best," Ellie promised.

As Ellie stood in front of the picture of
Queen Malice, it jeered at her. "So you
think you can get rid of me with a little
paint?" the picture mocked. "Let's see
you try!"

Trying to ignore the horrid queen,
Ellie dipped the thin brush into the black
paint, planning to draw an outline of
King Merry. But as she lifted the brush
and touched it to the canvas, her fingers
felt awkward and clumsy. The brush
slipped, leaving a messy black smudge.

"Oops!" said Ellie. Frowning, she
concentrated hard and tried to fix her
mistake, but every new line she painted
seemed to make it worse. Her picture
of King Merry ended up looking like a
drawing of a stick man!

"I don't know what's happening," Ellie

said, turning to the others in dismay.
"Even Molly could draw a better picture
than this."

Queen Malice's
face stared out of
the painting and
cackled. "Oh
dear. Not as
talented as you
thought you were."

Jasmine groaned as
she realised what was happening. "It's
your bracelet. Queen Malice said they
would take our talents away. It must
have taken away your talent for art!"

Ellie felt tears prickle her eyes. She
hated not being able to paint. And she
hated not being able to help Jasper.
"What are we going to do?" she asked.

"Trixi, can you try using your magic to break the spell," suggested Summer.

Trixi tapped her ring. Nothing happened. Trixi frowned and tapped her ring again.

Still nothing.

"My magic's not working!" she said in dismay.

"Oh, Trixi," said Summer, "Your bracelet must have taken away your talent for doing magic!"

Trixi gulped. "But I'm a royal pixie. I have to use my magic!"

Ellie looked at Jasmine and Summer's black bracelets. "What talents have your bracelets taken away?" she wondered aloud.

"I bet I can guess," Jasmine said grimly. *"Twinkle, twinkle, little star,"* she sang, but her voice sounded so croaky and out of tune that her friends had to

cover their ears. Rising onto her tiptoes, she tried to do a twirl but fell on her bottom. The paintings all pointed at her and laughed nastily.

Climbing back to her feet, Jasmine sighed. "I bet I can't play any instruments, either."

Ellie felt so sorry for her friend. She was normally such a graceful dancer and talented singer. Music meant as much to Jasmine as art meant to her and animals meant to Summer. Ellie gasped as she realised what talent Summer had probably lost.

Summer walked slowly over to the griffin statue. "Yikes!" she cried, jumping back as the griffin tried to peck her with its beak and swipe her with its claws.

"What's the matter?" taunted the

picture of Queen Malice. "The cute little griffin isn't your friend any more? Good! No other animals will like you, either."

Furious, Ellie pulled off her painting smock and hung it over the picture of the queen. At least now they wouldn't have to see her!

"I'm so sorry that my sister has stolen your talents," cried King Merry. "And poor, dear Jasper." He turned to look at the Jasper statue, whose moustache drooped sadly. "I just don't see how the Sparkle Statue ceremony can go ahead now."

"We've stopped Queen Malice before and we'll do it again," declared Jasmine.

"That's right," said Summer. "Even without our talents, we'll try everything we can to break the curse."

"The award ceremony must go ahead," Ellie said, looking over at the statue of Jasper. "We can't let Jasper down."

"Thank you, my dear friends," said King Merry. "I know I can always count on you. I'll go back to the palace and get the Sparkle Statue." He frowned and scratched his curly hair. "But how can I get there?"

"I can't magic you there," Trixi said. "But you can go through a painting."

"Good thinking,

Trixi!" said King Merry.

The girls were all confused. "What do you mean?" asked Summer.

"Remember how Queen Malice jumped out of the painting," explained Trixi. "Well, you can jump into an illusion painting, too. It takes you to the place it shows."

King Merry ran over to a picture of the Enchanted Palace. "I'll be back as soon as I can, dear friends. Please do everything you can to break the spell here!"

"We will!" the girls promised.

"Thank you!" With a worried look,
King Merry jumped into the picture of
the Enchanted Palace.

There was a bright
glow of light and
the little king
disappeared.
Amazed, the
girls saw him
appear in
the picture
and hurry in
through the
palace gates.
"That's
incredible!"
breathed Ellie.

"Quick, girls!" Trixi urged, flying around their heads. "There's no time to waste. How are we going to break the spell?"

"Maybe *we* can fix the painting?" suggested Summer. "I know we're not as good as you, Ellie, but perhaps you could tell us what to do – like you did when we were doing our pictures back at home."

"OK," said Ellie. "It's worth a try."

The art imps handed the palette and brushes to Summer and Jasmine. They had just dipped brushes into the paint when they heard a sinister flapping of wings.

Five dark shapes came swooping in through the museum's open doors. They had grey bodies, big ears, bat-like wings and beady eyes.

"Oh no, just what we need!" Summer groaned. "Storm Sprites!"

Under Attack!

"Queen Malice tricked you!" the sprites shrieked. "Ha, ha, ha!"

"Go away, you horrible things!" Jasmine shouted at Queen Malice's mean servants.

"No!" they jeered. "We've come to make this museum really miserable! Let's start with the statues."

They flapped over to the griffin statue. "Come on!" they cried. "Up you get!" The griffin stepped off its pedestal and started flapping around the gallery, pecking at paintings with its sharp eagle's beak. Summer ducked as it tried to peck at her! It was so different from the cute statue she'd met earlier.

Next the Storm Sprites flapped over to a statue of a Rainbow Lion. It leapt off its pedestal with a growl and started racing around the gallery, slashing at other statues with its claws.

"But the *real* Rainbow Lion is so kind and brave," Summer said in dismay, remembering the adventure they'd had finding the Secret Kingdom's Animal Keepers.

Then the Storm Sprites flew over to a

huge statue of a Dream Dragon. The Dream Dragon let out a ferocious roar and flew around the gallery, thrashing its long tail from side to side.

Jasmine couldn't believe what they were seeing. The Dream Dragons they'd met in Dream Dale were the gentlest creatures imaginable.

"Queen Malice's spell must be making all of the paintings and statues behave horribly," Ellie said.

One of the Storm Sprites spied Jasper's paint and paintbrushes. It grabbed a paintbrush and dunked it into red paint.

"Oooh! I'm really good at painting!" it screeched, then scrawled a moustache on a picture of a pretty fairy. The fairy fluttered furiously around the painting, wiping her mouth crossly.

Ellie couldn't bear to see Jasper's beautiful works of art ruined. "Stop that right now!" she said, trying to snatch the paintbrush away from the Storm Sprite.

"You can't stop us!" jeered the Storm Sprites.

They each pulled a fat, grey raindrop the size of a watermelon from under their wings.

"Misery drops!" cried Ellie in dismay. Whenever someone was hit by a misery drop they were left feeling too sad to do anything but sit and cry.

The sprites started to throw the drops at the girls, Trixi and the art imps.

"Silly girls!" the sprites taunted, throwing their misery drops at them.

SPLASH! SPLAT! The drops hit the floor, narrowly missing the girls and Trixi.

The girls ducked behind Jasper's statue. The artist was shaking his fist at the Storm Sprites as they flew overhead, laughing.

"How are we going to break the curse on the

museum and free Jasper if we can't repaint the portrait of King Merry?" said Jasmine.

"We need to get rid of the Storm Sprites," said Trixi.

"But how?" asked Jasmine.

Ellie suddenly thought of how King Merry had jumped into the painting. "I've got an idea!" she said.

"What is it?" said Summer.

"We'll make them think that we're statues – then trick them into jumping into a picture," explained Ellie.

"We'll have to act like the other statues, though," said Jasmine. "And they're being naughty because of Queen Malice's curse."

"Do you think it will work?" said
Summer.

Ellie grinned. "There's only one way to
find out!"

"I'll distract the Storm Sprites!" Trixi
volunteered. "I might not have my
magic, but I can still fly!"

The brave little pixie flew her leaf
into the middle of the room. "Hey, over
here!" she shouted. She sped into the next
room, the sprites flapping after her.

Ellie, Summer and Jasmine ran
and jumped onto three of the empty
pedestals. They all struck poses. Jasmine
stuck one leg out like a dancer. Ellie
lay down on her tummy and rested her
chin in her hand, as if she were deep in
thought. Summer put one hand on her
hip, and the other behind her head.

"Now try not to move," Ellie whispered to the others.

Moments later, the Storm Sprites followed Trixi back into the main gallery. Trixi flew her leaf over to the art imps and started talking loudly to them. "Look at the dreadful mess those

Storm Sprites have made. It's a shame they frightened away King Merry's special friends, but at least they haven't found his FAVOURITE STATUES."

"Yes," agreed the art imp with yellow hair, talking as loudly as possible so the Storm Sprites would hear. "The BRAND NEW STATUES of his Very Important Friends."

"Look! Statues of those horrible girls!" said one of the sprites, flapping over to where the girls were standing, pretending to be statues.

Jasmine tried not to move a muscle as the Storm Sprites stared at her. She was starting to get pins and needles in her foot!

"Yuck! They look just like they do in real life!" said another.

Ellie had to bite her lip to stop herself from giggling.

"But now they'll be rude and naughty!" crowed a third sprite.

Unable to stay still a second longer, Summer jumped off her pedestal and blew a raspberry at them.

Trying not to giggle, Jasmine stuck her tongue out at them. She dodged around the room, pretending to be a naughty statue come to life.

"After them!" the lead sprite called.

Jasmine ran around the museum, followed by two sprites.

"Over here!" Trixi shouted, hovering her leaf in front of a painting of Lily Pad Lake.

The girls all ran towards Trixi, the sprites flapping right behind them.

"We're going to catch you!" the sprites cackled, racing towards the girls with their spiky fingers outstretched. "We're going to get you and... EEK!"

When they reached the picture, Trixi and the girls jumped out of the way, but the sprites were going too fast to stop.

SPLASH!

They crashed into the picture – and fell right into Lily Pad Lake!

"Ugh! I'm soaked!" spluttered one of the Storm Sprites, thrashing about in the blue water.

"I'm cold!" cried one Storm Sprite, climbing out of the water. "I'm getting out of here!"

"Me too," said another, flying up into the air. "Let's go back home to Thunder Castle."

As the girls looked at the painting, they saw the bedraggled Storm Sprites flap off.

Summer grinned. "Phew! They've finally gone! Now we can fix the portrait and break the curse!"

Breaking the Curse

The art imps scurried over with paints and brushes. Summer and Jasmine each took a brush. Ellie wished she could paint too, but she knew the only thing she could do was try to help her friends. She took her smock off the portrait of Queen Malice.

"I don't know where to start," Summer said nervously.

"Me neither," said Jasmine.

The queen in the picture glared at
them. "Don't bother! You'll never make
this plan work!"

"Oh, be quiet!" Ellie waving the
paintbrush crossly.

"Gah!" Queen Malice
cried out.

Ellie looked up
and burst into
giggles. She'd
accidentally
flicked the brush
and green paint
had splattered
all over the horrid
queen's face!

Queen Malice gave an outraged shriek.
"How dare you!" she spluttered, wiping
paint out of her eyes. "You little—" But

before she could finish, Jasmine splashed white paint over the whole canvas.

"There! That's better!" Jasmine grinned.

"Now, we can work without her nasty comments distracting us," Ellie said. "Come on," she urged Summer and Jasmine. "You can do this. Just picture King Merry in your head and paint what you see."

Summer started to paint an outline of the king's head. Jasmine added some curly white hair.

"It's looking good. Remember what you did with the unicorn painting," Ellie said encouragingly.

Summer added some glitter to the king's crown, while Jasmine started to paint his bright blue eyes.

"If you use little flecks of white paint his eyes will look as if they're twinkling," suggested Ellie, thinking about King Merry's friendly face.

Trixi smiled. "King Merry's eyes always twinkle!"

Summer and Jasmine followed Ellie's instructions. After finishing King Merry's head and crown, they painted his plump body. It was the best painting they had ever done.

"It looks just like King Merry!" Ellie said happily. "You just need to add a touch of pink to his cheeks and some glittery highlights on his glasses to make them sparkle."

Summer and Jasmine quickly did as Ellie suggested.

"It looks really good!" Trixi said.

Ellie hugged Summer and Jasmine. "You've done a brilliant job."

"Only because you helped us," said Jasmine.

Summer looked around, hoping that Jasper had come back to life. But he was still a statue, his moustache drooping sadly as he looked down at the Art Imps. All the other statues were chasing each other around the museum, and the paintings were still dull shades of grey. "Why hasn't the spell broken?" she asked. "Queen Malice said the museum would be under her spell while her painting hung here. We fixed it, but nothing's changed."

With sinking hearts, Jasmine and Ellie realised she was right.

"I wonder if it's because you haven't

used Jasper's magic illusion brush yet,"
Trixi said suddenly. "Try using that."

Jasmine picked up the brush with the
shimmering bristles. "Shall I try?"

They nodded. Remembering what
Jasper had done, Jasmine brushed the
painting's surface with magic sparkles.
They all held their breath.

"A-a-a-a-CHOO!"

The portrait of King Merry came to
life as he sneezed. "Ooh, that
paintbrush tickled my

nose!" he chuckled.

CRACK! With a flash of light, Queen
Malice's spell was broken. The grey
cloud overhead vanished and sunlight
streamed in through the glass ceiling.
The statues had stopped being naughty
and returned to their pedestals and the
paintings were brightly coloured
and cheerful once more.

"Quick! Look,
something's

happening to Jasper!" cried Trixi.

The air around Jasper was shimmering with magic, and the golden stone crumbed into tiny pieces. As Jasper stepped out of the shards and dust, his moustache changed from an angry red to a deep blue. "Oh, thank you! Thank you!" he cried to Ellie. "You managed to paint King Merry and break the curse!"

"Well, actually, I didn't. It was my friends. They painted the new portrait of King Merry." Ellie held up her bracelet sadly. "I can't paint any more. My talent has all gone, thanks to Queen Malice."

Jasper shook his head in dismay. "You can't paint… Oh no, you poor child."

"You *did* help break the curse, Ellie," said Summer. "We only managed to paint the picture because you told us what to do."

"And you were the one who thought of the plan to get rid of the Storm Sprites," Jasmine said. She put her arms round Ellie and Summer. "We broke the curse together!"

"Girls! King Merry's coming!" cried Trixi, zooming over to the museum's entrance on her leaf.

Jasmine, Summer and Ellie ran to the door. King Merry was sliding down a rainbow that had magically appeared in the sky. He was clutching a sparkling statue that shimmered with as many colours as Jasper's moustache. A crowd of elves, brownies and pixies squealed as they tumbled down the rainbow after him.

King Merry somersaulted off the end
of the slide and flew through the air.
"Whoa!" he cried.

Trixi gasped and tapped her pixie ring:

"When King Merry flies up aloft,
Let him land on something soft."

She chanted. But of course her magic
wasn't working. No magic sparkles came
out of her ring.

"Watch out!" she cried in alarm as the
king fell towards the ground.

A golden trampoline suddenly appeared
underneath the king. He bounced several
times on it.

"How did that happen?" Trixi gasped.

"Hello, Trixi." An elegant older pixie
swooped over on her leaf.

"Aunt Maybelle!" cried Trixi.

Aunt Maybelle was Trixi's great aunt and one of the most powerful pixies in the land. "I love Jasper's paintings," she said. "So, I decided to come along to the award ceremony."

"Thank you," Trixi said in relief. "King Merry, are you OK?" she asked, whooshing over to the king.

King Merry struggled to stand upright on the trampoline. His crown had slipped to one side, but he was still clutching the Sparkle Statue. "I'm fine. Is everyone else all right?" he gasped.

"Yes, Your Majesty!" Trixi said. "The girls broke the spell on the museum and now it's all back to normal."

Summer, Jasmine and Ellie ran over to help King Merry off the trampoline.

"Thank you so much, girls," King Merry said. Then he saw that they were still wearing their black bracelets. "Oh no! I was hoping the curse on your talents would have broken, too. Maybe we should delay the ceremony and try to get your talents back."

Ellie shook her head. "No," she said. "That wouldn't be fair to Jasper."

Jasmine nodded. "Or all the people who've come to the museum."

"The Sparkle Statue ceremony must go on!" said Summer.

The Sparkle Statue

Everyone gathered around the new
painting of King Merry. Even the
pictures fell quiet as King Merry walked
to the front of the gallery with Jasper.
King Merry held up the glittering
award. Jasper Rococo's name magically
appeared on the statue in fancy lettering.

"Ahem! As you all know, it's Talent Week," King Merry announced. "The Sparkle Statue is awarded to someone whose talent has brought lots of beauty and sparkle to the Secret Kingdom. Jasper, your wonderful paintings bring such happiness to the whole realm! It is with enormous pleasure that I present you with this award."

In a flurry of magical sparkles, the statue flew through the air and into Jasper's hands. Everyone clapped and cheered as loudly as they could.

Jasper was so overcome with joy that his moustache turned a deep, rosy pink. He bowed deeply. "Thank you, Your Majesty. Thank you, everyone. I am honoured to accept the Sparkle Statue."

Suddenly, the statue flashed brightly

and suddenly Jasper started to glow and shimmer all over.

The crowd gasped. Even Jasper looked surprised. "What's happening?" he asked King Merry.

The little king looked flustered. He scratched his head. "Oh dear. Now what did I forget to mention…"

Aunt Maybelle coughed gently. "Does the award grant any special powers, King Merry?" she reminded him.

"Ah yes!" cried King Merry. "That's it! When my great grandfather set up Talent Week thousands of years ago, he made each of the prizes magic. The Sparkle Statue will heighten your artistic talent for one whole day. You can keep the power to yourself or share it with others if you prefer."

Jasper beamed. "I would like to share it." He paused and twirled his moustache thoughtfully. "I wonder... if I can share my talent with anyone... what will happen if I share it with you?" He looked at Ellie. "You have had your talent for art taken away and yet you still came up with the plan that saved me. Without the advice you gave your friends, I would still be a statue."

Ellie felt everyone look at her. She swallowed and walked over to Jasper, her heart beating fast. Would the magic let her draw and paint again?

The crowd watched anxiously as Jasper touched the Sparkle Statue to the bracelet on Ellie's wrist. Suddenly there was the sound of a thunderbolt breaking.

Ellie gasped as the bracelet turned from black back to purple. Now the bracelet was even prettier than before, with silver and gold woven into the lilac threads. Jasper stepped back.

"Let us see if your talent has returned!" Jasper said. He handed Ellie one of his paintbrushes and said, "Add something to the portrait of King Merry."

Ellie walked slowly over to the painting. What could she paint? What if the award's magic hadn't worked? She smiled to herself as she suddenly realised what was missing from the picture. Of course!

She dipped the end of the brush into the green paint and began to draw someone standing on a leaf. She dabbed the brush in yellow paint, adding messy

blonde hair. Then she painted a silver
dress, dainty shoes, and a little hat
shaped like a daisy. As a final touch, she
added a dot of glitter to the bright blue
eyes. "There," she said, stepping back so
everyone could see what she had done.

"It's Trixi!" cried Summer and Jasmine.

Trixi's cheeks
turned pink with
delight. "Oh!"
she exclaimed,
turning a loop-
the-loop in the
air. "It looks
just like me!"

"Wonderful!
Quite
wonderful!"
said King Merry.

"That was exactly what the portrait needed! Thank you, Ellie!'

Jasper put his arm round Ellie's shoulders. "Your talent has returned."

Everyone cheered.

Ellie glanced at her friends. The bracelets around their wrists were still black and horrid.

"I'm sorry you still don't have your talents," she said miserably.

"It's OK." Summer gave her a hug. "We're happy you've got yours back."

"And at least we know how to break the spell now," Jasmine said practically. "If we award the talent show prizes then we can use their power to get our own talents back!"

King Merry clapped his hands. "That's sorted then! You must join us for the

rest of the ceremonies, and we'll undo
my sister's spell! But for now, everyone,
please enjoy the museum!"

The elves, brownies and pixies dashed
off to look at the paintings. Soon
laughter and lively talk filled the bright
gallery as people wandered around
chatting with the pictures and stroking
the statues. Some brownie musicians
struck up a lively tune.

"Let's dance!" Jasmine cried. She spun

round, but tripped over her feet and landed in a heap on the floor. "Oh," she said, biting her lip. "I forgot that I can't."

The girls went over to the statue of the griffin. It jumped off its pedestal and nuzzled Ellie. "Aw! He's adorable," Ellie said, patting him.

Jasmine ruffled the griffin's golden feathers and he let out a happy coo. But when Summer crouched down and tried to stroke the little creature, he cowered behind Jasmine and Ellie.

Summer sighed and looked down at her cursed bracelet. "It's so sad that animals are scared of me."

Ellie hugged her friends. "We *will* get your talents back. Together we can do anything. You know we can."

"You're right," said Jasmine, staring down at the black bracelet around her wrist. "Queen Malice has never beaten us before and she's not going to do it now, either."

Trixi flew over on her leaf. "Aunt Maybelle is going to have to do the magic to send you home today. It's so annoying not being able to use my magic," she sighed.

Aunt Maybelle smiled. "We'll send you a message as soon as it's time for the next ceremony."

Trixi flew up and kissed them each on the nose.

"Bye, Trixi," they chorused.

"Goodbye, my friends," said the king. "We'll see you soon."

"Are you ready?" Aunt Maybelle asked.

They nodded and she tapped her pixie ring. Glittering silver sparkles surrounded the girls and whisked them away. Their feet hit the ground with a gentle thump and they found themselves back in Ellie's kitchen with the Magic Box at their feet.

"Wow, what an adventure!" Ellie said.

"And it's just the start," said Jasmine. She looked down at her bracelet. "We must keep an eye on the Magic Box."

"We have to break the spell on these bracelets," Summer said. She picked up the Magic Box and slipped it back into her backpack – and only just in time.

The kitchen door opened. "What are you doing?" asked Molly.

"Just playing a game," said Ellie.

"A *secret* game," said Jasmine.

Summer hid her grin.

"Did you find my glitter gel pens?" Ellie asked her sister.

"Yes!" Molly showed Ellie her picture. "But I can't get the fairy's wings right."

"Here, I'll help." Ellie dipped a brush into the paint on the table and added some delicate wings to her sister's picture.

"Thank you!" Molly said happily. She gave Ellie a big hug. "Now it looks perfect!"

Ellie felt a warm glow. She looked down at the purple bracelet on her wrist. It would always remind her how very lucky she was to be able to draw and paint so well.

Ellie smiled at Summer and Jasmine.

Soon they would be off to the Secret Kingdom again, and she'd do everything she could to make sure her friends got their special talents back too!

Read on for a sneak peek of the next exciting Secret Kingdom adventure,

Melody Medal

Read on for a sneak peek...

A Message from Trixi

"Did your grandma and grandpa have a good time on their cruise, Jasmine?" asked Summer Hammond.

"They said it was fantastic!" replied her friend, Jasmine Smith. She ran to her wardrobe and took out a grass skirt. "Look – they bought me this in Hawaii," she said, pulling it on over her jeans. "And this." She clipped a purple silk orchid into her long black hair.

"Wow!" said Ellie Macdonald, Jasmine and Summer's other best friend.

The three friends were in Jasmine's bedroom. She'd invited Summer and Ellie over to see the lovely gifts her grandparents had brought back from their trip.

"Hawaiian traditional dancing looks a bit like this," Jasmine said. She swung her hips, setting the grass skirt rustling, and moved her hands from side to side with a chuckle. "It's called *hula* dancing. My grandparents showed me a video."

"That looks great, Jasmine," Summer said with a smile. "I'd love to go to Hawaii."

"Me too," said Jasmine dreamily,

and then pointed to her bedside table. "Grandma and Grandpa sent me that postcard while they were there, and they showed me all their photos. Hawaii looks *brilliant*."

Ellie picked up the postcard. "Look at that beach," she sighed. "And those palm trees. It really would be amazing to go there."

"Yes, it would," agreed Summer. She grinned at Ellie and Jasmine. "But we already have an amazing place to visit!"

The girls exchanged excited looks, thinking about the wonderful secret that they shared. They looked after a magic box that could take them to the Secret Kingdom, a beautiful place ruled by kind King Merry. They'd had lots of adventures there, and had met unicorns, brownies, elves, imps and many other magical creatures.

"I hope we can get back to the Secret Kingdom soon," Jasmine said. "Especially with all the trouble Queen Malice is causing there." She and Summer looked anxiously at their wrists. Queen Malice, King Merry's nasty sister, had tricked them and their pixie friend, Trixi, into wearing friendship bracelets that had stolen their talents. The once-colourful bracelets had been turned into dull black metal. Luckily Ellie's talent for art had been magically returned during their last adventure there, and so her bracelet had turned back to a pretty purple band with a silver paintbrush charm. But Jasmine's talent for dancing and music and Summer's talent for making friends with animals would be missing until they broke the bracelets' spell.

"At least we've still got our talents when we're at home," said Ellie. "But poor Trixi lives in the Secret Kingdom and can't use her magic at all."

"We have to help her get it back," Summer said. "So we've *got* to go back there."

"And we've got to stop Queen Malice from wrecking the Talent Week events," said Jasmine. Talent Week was an ancient Secret Kingdom tradition, and it was taking place in the magical realm that week. King Merry was presenting four awards to people who used their special skills to help the Secret Kingdom. Each time an award was given out, Summer, Jasmine and Trixi would have

a chance to get their lost talents back –
but Queen Malice was trying to stop that
from happening so she could take over
the kingdom without the girls getting in
her way. If they didn't get their talents
back by the end of the week, they'd be
lost forever!

"I wish we could go to the Secret
Kingdom right this minute," Summer
said wistfully.

"Me too," agreed Ellie. She opened her
backpack and looked inside it, hoping to
see the Magic Box glowing. When there
was a message from their friends in the
Secret Kingdom, the mirror set into the
box's curved lid lit up. But there wasn't
even a glimmer of light coming from
it now. "No message from Trixi," she
sighed.

"I'm sure we'll hear from her soon," said Summer, but she was disappointed, too. She couldn't wait to get back her talent with animals. Being in the Secret Kingdom wasn't the same without it.

"Don't look so gloomy," said Jasmine. "I think I know how to cheer us all up." She picked up a ukulele that was leaning against the foot of her bed. It was made of pale wood and looked like a tiny guitar. "Grandma and Grandpa brought this back for me, too! I'll play a tune."

Summer and Ellie sat on Jasmine's bed and listened eagerly while Jasmine strummed out a cheerful tune. Summer clapped in time to the music and Ellie tapped her foot on the floor.

"That was great, Jasmine!" they exclaimed together, when she'd finished.

"Thanks," said Jasmine, smiling. "It's funny playing such a cute little instrument. It feels sort of magical – a bit like being in the Secret Kingdom!"

"I'm glad the friendship bracelets don't take our talents away when we're here," Summer said. "If they did..." She didn't get a chance to finish because Ellie gave a loud whoop. "The Magic Box!" she cried. "It's glowing!"

She pulled the box out of her backpack and they all gathered around it excitedly. The sides of the box were beautifully carved with mermaids, unicorns and other amazing creatures, and the mirror on the lid was surrounded by six glittering green gems.

"Here comes the message," said Jasmine eagerly, as silvery letters began

to appear in the mirror. The letters
formed into sparkling words that snaked
up out of the mirror and floated up into
the air. Jasmine read them out:

"Surrounded by blue twinkling sea,
This island's as quiet as quiet can be.
There's peace and happiness,
calm and hush
And life is slow. No need to rush!"

Read
Melody Medal
to find out what
happens next!

Have you read all the books in Series Six?

Sparkle Statue

ROSIE BANKS

Melody Medal

ROSIE BANKS

Pet Show Prize

ROSIE BANKS

Twinkle Trophy

ROSIE BANKS

Can Summer, Jasmine, Ellie and Trixi
defeat Queen Malice and get their talents
back before Talent Week is over?

Oh no! Jasmine's lost her talent for music – can you help her break the curse by finding her way to her instruments? But watch out for mean old Queen Malice!

Secret Kingdom

Competition!

Would you like to win one of three Secret Kingdom goody bags?

All you have to do is design and create your own friendship bracelet just like Ellie, Summer and Jasmine's!

Here is how to enter:

* Visit www.secretkingdombooks.com
* Click on the competition page at the top
* Print out the bracelet activity sheet and decorate it
* Once you've made your bracelet send your entry into us

The lucky winners will receive an extra special Secret Kingdom goody bag full of treats and activities.

Please send entries to:
Secret Kingdom Friendship Bracelet Competition
Orchard Books, 338 Euston Road, London, NW1 3BH

Don't forget to add your name and address.

Good luck!

Closing dates:
There are three chances to win
before the closing date on the 30th October 2015

Secret Kingdom

A magical world of
friendship and fun!

Join the Secret Kingdom Club at

www.secretkingdombooks.com

and enjoy games, sneak peeks and lots more!

You'll find great activities, competitions, stories
and games, plus a special newsletter for
Secret Kingdom friends!